SHAKESPEARE RETOLD

MACBETH

by

Martin Waddell & Alan Marks

First published in 2008
by Franklin Watts
338 Euston Road
London NW1 3BH

Franklin Watts Australia
Level 17/207 Kent Street
Sydney NSW 2000

Editor: Jackie Hamley
Series Designer: Peter Scoulding

ISBN: 978 0 7496 7742 8 (hbk)
ISBN: 978 0 7496 7748 0 (pbk)

Printed in China

Fnanklin Watts is a divisic
Hachette Children's Book
an Hachette Livre UK co
www.hachettelivre.co.uk

CONTENTS

THE CAST

Three witches

King Duncan – King of Scotland
Malcolm – Duncan's son
Donalbain – Duncan's son

Banquo – General to King Duncan
Macduff – Thane of Fife
Macbeth – Thane of Glamis,
General to King Duncan

Lady Macbeth – Wife to Macbeth
Lady Macduff – Wife to Macduff

A doctor, a messenger, a watchman,
two murderers and many soldiers

PROLOGUE

A battle on a barren moor,
three witches and a bloodsoaked room.
A murdered king, a butchered friend,
a ghastly ghost and lots of gore.
Trees that walk, a fierce revenge,
a severed head...

...this is the story of Macbeth.

CHAPTER ONE

ENTER THREE WITCHES

Two trusted generals, Macbeth and Banquo, found themselves alone on a barren moor after a fierce battle. The two friends had fought together and defeated a rebel army, saving the throne of Scotland for Duncan, their king. Victorious, they were trudging home, bloodstained and battle weary.

Suddenly a strange mist swirled round them. Out of the mist came three dreadful witches, rejoicing in the blood and hate of battle.

"Hail Macbeth, Thane of Glamis!
Hail Macbeth, Thane of Cawdor!
Hail Macbeth, who shall be king!"
they cackled.

Macbeth was Thane of Glamis already,
but the witches' words were carefully chosen.
Hail Macbeth, who shall be king…
The witches were tempting Macbeth with
thoughts of the glory that could be his.

The witches turned to Banquo. "You will not be so great as Macbeth, yet you will be greater," they told him. "Not so happy, yet much happier. You will not be king, but your sons will be kings!"

The mist swirled and the witches vanished.
"Don't trust witches," Banquo warned Macbeth.
"Their words do not mean what they seem to."

King, thought Macbeth, *I shall be king.*

Then a messenger from King Duncan arrived.
"Hail Macbeth, Thane of Cawdor!" the
messenger cried.

Thane of Cawdor, thought Macbeth.

The Thane of Cawdor had been one of
the rebels. As a reward for the great victory,
King Duncan had named Macbeth Thane of
Cawdor in the traitor's place.

I am Thane of Cawdor as the witches promised,
thought Macbeth. *So could I be king?*

CHAPTER TWO

A BLOODY DEED

"The witches promised that I would be king!" Macbeth wrote to his wife. "How can that be, while Duncan sits safe on his throne?"

Why should the husband I love not be king? thought Lady Macbeth, as she read his letter. *He could be king... if he really wanted to be. If only I could find the willpower to drive him on. If only I could borrow the power of the witches.*

"King Duncan will sleep here tonight!" Macbeth told his wife on his return.

"Kill Duncan and you will be king in his place," she said, spelling out what had to be done.

"But Duncan trusts me," Macbeth said, confused between his loyalty to the king and his own burning ambition.

"If you want it enough, you will do it!" cried Lady Macbeth, challenging the man she loved. "If I were a man, I would do it myself!"

That night, urged on by his wife,
Macbeth crept up to Duncan's
bedchamber. A vision of a dagger
dripped blood before his horrified eyes.
He reached for it, but the dagger vanished,
disappearing into his troubled mind. Macbeth
struggled with evil... and lost.

Lady Macbeth had already drugged King
Duncan's servants who now lay fast asleep.
No one stopped Macbeth as he stabbed
the sleeping king again and again.

There was blood everywhere.
Lady Macbeth smeared it all over the
drugged servants so that they would
be blamed for Duncan's murder.

Next morning one of the
nobles, Macduff, discovered the king's
body and the bloodstained servants.

"Traitors!" howled Macbeth, blaming them for the
murder. Ranting about their treachery, he slit the
servants' throats before they could be questioned.

The nobles proclaimed Macbeth king, in place of the man he had murdered.

Macduff was suspicious of Macbeth, and made his escape from the castle. Duncan's sons, Malcolm and Donalbain, also fled fearing that they would be next to die.

"King Duncan's sons had their father murdered by the servants so that they could seize the throne!" Macbeth declared when he learned of their flight.

CHAPTER THREE

A GHOSTLY GUEST

Macbeth was King of Scotland as the witches had promised, but he was troubled. Any one of his nobles might turn against him, and kill as he had killed to seize the throne.

"Banquo's sons will be kings hereafter!" the witches had said. That meant only one thing to Macbeth. He had murdered to gain his throne... now he would have to kill Banquo to save it.

"My mind is full of scorpions!" he told his wife. "I cannot sleep."

"Keep calm," she said. "You are king. Who can threaten you?"

Banquo thought Macbeth.

Macbeth invited Banquo and his son to a great feast and arranged for them to be killed as they journeyed to his castle. They were ambushed, and Banquo was hacked to death.

"Banquo is dead… but his son got away," one of the hired murderers whispered to Macbeth. *Let the son escape,* Macbeth thought. He could deal with the son later. It was his old friend Banquo he had feared most… and now feared no more, for Banquo was dead.

Macbeth made a king's entrance to the dining hall, striding to his place at the table, joking and laughing. But...

Bloody and horrible, Banquo's ghost sat in Macbeth's chair glowering at the man who had had him butchered.

"You dare not say I did it!" Macbeth shouted pointing at the ghost... but only he could see the bloody beckoning figure.
The nobles saw only the empty chair.

Seeing the terror in
her husband's face, Lady
Macbeth was afraid. Screaming
and out of control, he might blurt
out the truth in front of the nobles and
lose all that she had helped him win.

"My husband is ill," she told the guests, dragging
him to one side. "He has fits like this sometimes.
It means nothing."

"Be a man!" she whispered to Macbeth. "There is no one in your chair."

"Banquo is there, drippping blood," Macbeth sobbed.

"There is no one there!" Lady Macbeth insisted.

Macbeth turned and saw that the chair was empty.

"Act normally," Lady Macbeth told him.

Macbeth tried to obey. He came back to the table, cheerfully proposing a toast... he raised his glass... and there was the ghost again, blood smearing his clothes, great gobs of it caught in his hair, beckoning at Macbeth.

Macbeth screamed with fear. Lady Macbeth took charge at once. She ordered the others to leave, but the damage was done.

The nobles had heard what she had heard, and seen what she had seen… their king cowering guiltily before an empty chair.

FOUR VISIONS

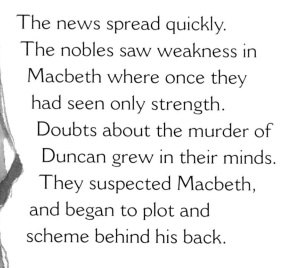

The news spread quickly. The nobles saw weakness in Macbeth where once they had seen only strength. Doubts about the murder of Duncan grew in their minds. They suspected Macbeth, and began to plot and scheme behind his back.

Lady Macbeth was frightened. She knew that she could no longer control what her husband said or did. She pleaded with him when they were alone, but Macbeth wouldn't listen to her anymore.

Instead Macbeth sought the witches' help, entering the darkness of their cave alone.

"Double double, toil and trouble, fire burn and cauldron bubble!" the three hags cackled, gloating at Macbeth's return. The visions they conjured in the foul smelling smoke from their magic cauldron were to deceive him once again.

A head in a warrior's helmet appeared first, grinning at him. "Beware Macduff!" the head warned.

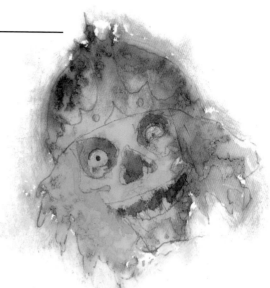

I know how to deal with Macduff, Macbeth told himself. What was another murder to him, when he'd killed before?

Next came a child, dripping with blood. "No man of woman born can harm Macbeth!" the child said.

No one can harm me! thought Macbeth.

Then a vision of a second child came forward.

It held a small tree in its hands. "Macbeth will never be defeated till Birnam Wood shall come to Dunsinane!" it said.

Trees don't walk thought Macbeth. *I can never be defeated.*

Once again, he believed what the witches wanted him to believe.

"What of your promises
to Banquo?" Macbeth
asked the witches.
Macbeth was king.
How could Banquo's
sons inherit his throne?

In answer, a vision of
the murdered Banquo
appeared followed by
one king and then
another, and another... his
son, and his son's sons...
all kings to come.

A parade of kings... and
then they were gone...
all gone... the visions,
and the witches.

What could Macbeth do
but cling to the hope
the witches' promises
had given him, and make
sure that he dealt with
Macduff?

Beware Macduff... but by
now Macduff had fled to
England to join Duncan's
son, Malcolm, and raise
an army to fight
Macbeth.

"Kill Macduff's wife
and children anyway!"
the ruthless Macbeth
told his men.

CHAPTER FIVE

TREES THAT WALK

So brutal was the slaughter of Macduff's family that even Lady Macbeth was horrified. The ghosts of those Macbeth had murdered screamed in her mind, driving her mad. In her guilt and despair she walked and talked in her sleep.

"Who would have thought the old man had so much blood in him?" she sobbed. She kept trying to wash Duncan's blood off her hands. She saw blood and smelt blood, though the blood existed only in her mind.

Meanwhile, Macbeth's half-mad rantings and killings were turning men against him. The nobles deserted to join Macduff and Malcolm, who were advancing into Scotland with an army to overthrow Macbeth.

Macbeth was trapped with his enemies moving closer. How could he think about his wife and her madness?

"Cure her!" he told the doctor.

But no medicine could cure the despair in her soul. Lady Macbeth died.

Why must she die now when I have to face my enemies? Macbeth groaned, when they told him of her death. His world was collapsing around him, but he fought back.

No man born of woman can kill me! he told himself. *I cannot be defeated, until Birnam Wood comes to my castle walls at Dunsinane!*

Then... "My lord, the woods of Birnam walk!" an amazed watchman told Macbeth.

It cannot be! Trees don't walk!
Macbeth told himself.

But the trees *were* walking.

Macduff's and Malcolm's men had cut
leafy branches from the trees in
Birnam Wood. They held them above
their heads so that Macbeth's soldiers
could not tell how many were marching.
It looked as if the whole forest
was moving.

"Birnam Wood
has come to
Dunsinane!" swore
Macbeth. He still had
one hope left.

*No man of woman born
can harm Macbeth.*

Trapped by his enemies,
the warrior in Macbeth
took over.

He would not wait
to die. He would fight.
He was invincible.
He could never be
defeated.

"Follow me!" roared
Macbeth, drawing his
sword.

Macbeth led his men out through the castle gates in a desperate charge against his enemies, hacking and cutting at them with his mighty sword.

He waded in blood, using his terrible strength, cutting and killing his way through the enemy until...

He faced Macduff, the man whose wife and children he had put to the sword, the man who had good reason to hate him.

Something stirred within Macbeth, some knowledge of the terrible things he had done: the killing of Duncan; the murder of Banquo; the dreadful deaths of Macduff's wife and children.

Many had died so that Macbeth could be king…
must there be more?

"I killed your wife and children!" he pleaded
with his greatest enemy. "Don't make me kill
you too!"

"I leave my talking to my sword!" Macduff
answered fiercely.

"No man can kill me!" Macbeth warned
him. "If you fight me, you will die. No man
of woman born can harm me."

"No man of woman born?" said Macduff,
drawing his sword. "I was not born as most
men are, but taken from my mother's body
before the time for my birth had come.
I should have died… and yet I lived… and
live… to avenge my wife and children!"

They fought, and Macbeth lost.

Macduff held high the severed head of
Macbeth, a man who had killed all the good
that once lay in him, driven beyond all reason
to fulfil his ambition to be king.

In time Banquo's son came to the throne,
and his son's sons were all kings, just
as the witches
had predicted.

EPILOGUE

A battle on a barren moor,
three witches and a bloodsoaked room.
A murdered king, a butchered friend,
a ghastly ghost and lots of gore.
Trees that walk, a fierce revenge,
a severed head...

So ends the story of Macbeth.

NOTES

by Dr Catherine Alexander

Macbeth is based on real historical people and events, and Shakespeare took many of the details of the plot of the play from a history book by Raphael Holinshed, *Chronicles of England, Scotland and Ireland*. He then added actions, such as the banquet when Macbeth sees Banquo's ghost and Lady Macbeth sleepwalking, to make it more exciting. But as well as being about the past, Shakespeare also wanted to comment on the times he lived in.

Queen Elizabeth I, the last of the Tudor monarchs, died in 1603 and was succeeded by James, the first Stuart king of England, who already ruled Scotland. James enjoyed plays and entertainments and became patron of Shakespeare's theatre company, which was then given a new name – the King's Men.

Many people believe that when Shakespeare wrote *Macbeth*, probably in 1606, it was as a tribute to King James. The play is set in Scotland, James' homeland, and James claimed he was descended from the character Banquo. James was interested in witchcraft too – he had even written a book about it, called *Demonologie*, in 1597.

Legend has it that when James watched the play and the witches showed Macbeth the vision of eight kings, the last of the kings held up a mirror and pointed it at James – the ninth Stuart King of Scotland – so he could see himself reflected as the next in line to the throne.

But the play is also about rebellion and traitors – a problem in 1606. In 1605 Guy Fawkes and his companions had tried to blow up Parliament (in the Gunpowder Plot that is remembered every 5th November on Bonfire Night). King James was worried about threats to his safety: both his parents had died violently and he wore specially padded clothes in case he was attacked. He must have been pleased that at the end of the play the tyrant Macbeth, who murdered King Duncan, was overthrown.

Macbeth is still read and performed over four hundred years after it was written because we don't need to know about King James or to believe in witches to be interested in wickedness. Shakespeare writes about a good man, an excellent soldier who has done great service to his country, who turns bad. Why does this happen? Is it his ambition? Is he a weak man who is influenced by his strong wife or his belief in the supernatural? And what about Lady Macbeth? She tries to act tough but her actions drive her mad and her doctor cannot save her.

Shakespeare explores the causes and effects of bad deeds – how one evil thought or action leads to another – so that eventually the people who commit the deeds are themselves destroyed. It is a moral tale and, as the world still has violent tyrants, it is a tale that we can understand today.

MACBETH FACTS

❖ In Shakespeare's day, all the parts in a play were acted by boys or men. Nobody knows what the witches looked like or how they showed their visions but they have been played in lots of different ways. In 1671 a new London theatre used machinery to create special effects that allowed the witches to fly.

✤ *Macbeth* was first performed at the Globe, the open-air theatre on the south bank of the River Thames in London which was rebuilt in 1997.

✤ Lady Macbeth became a popular role and when Ellen Terry played the part in a famous production in London in 1888 her dress was decorated with real beetles' wings to make it shine.

✤ After a number of accidents in the theatre during performances of *Macbeth* many actors became superstitious and decided that it was unlucky to speak the title of the play out loud so instead refer to it as 'The Scottish Play'.

✤ There are over forty references to blood in the play and it can be very frightening: when Ian McKellen and Judi Dench performed *Macbeth* in Stratford in 1976 some of the audience held crosses to ward off evil.